CASEY BOHN

PRESENTS

PRESIDENT X

AND OTHER TALES OF DOOM AND GLOOM

Good Pals Publishing
White River Junction, Vermont

Good Pals Publishing
White River Junction, Vermont

CONTENTS

PRESIDENT X

Casey Bohn

PRESIDENT X

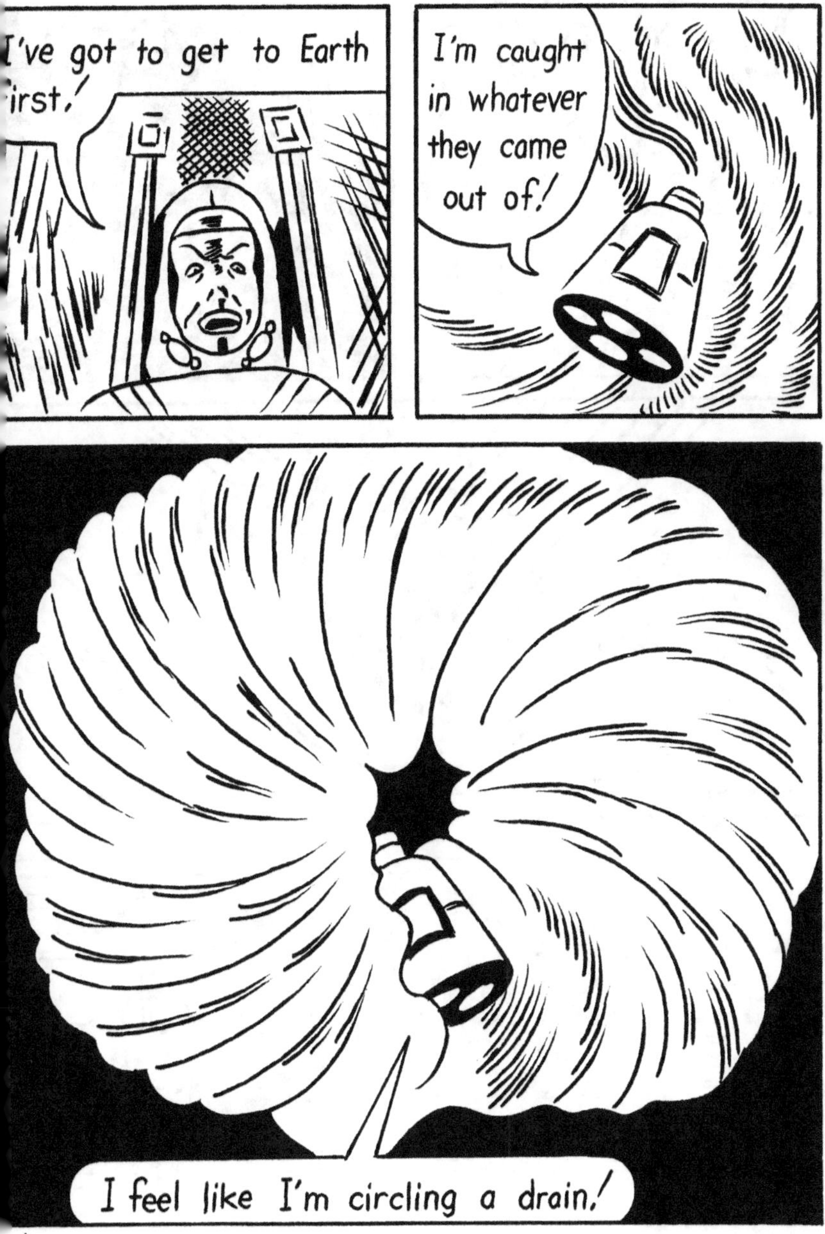

I feel like I'm circling a drain!

Casey Bohn

PRESIDENT X

Flynn, you've been lost in space for five years.

Things have changed — Things you must understand!

You need to come with us.

Casey Bohn

PRESIDENT X

Casey Bohn

PRESIDENT X

...ow you were asking about ...place for those with no ...ith in the Man.

I'm going to a place just like that.

...'s a *major* happening, man!

Everyone who's tuned in, turned off and dropped out will be there.

Is that so?

As my hair is long.

Yeah...

Casey Bohn

I've got nothing to lose. I'll join you.

Far out, a real spacehead on our side!

It smells awful.

Then we must be here!

What's that big tent for?

That's Gama Eave — hippie royalty!

He's psychic like you wouldn't believe.

Casey Bohn

A spaceship...

...but not your own...

...with eight aliens...

...and our *President* on board.

Holy sardine, you ARE psychic!

PRESIDENT X

More surprising to me...

...You've proven the President is controlled by space aliens.

And I'm the only man on Earth who can see the proof in your head.

What should we do?

Let me meditate on that.

While I do, try to make yourself comfortable.

Casey Bohn

PRESIDENT X

lacklight tent!... How can ght be black.?

BLACKLIGHT TENT

Woah....!

POOF!

Human. I have an offer to make.

Casey Bohn

PRESIDENT X

PRESIDENT X

Casey Bohn

PRESIDENT X

And this surprises you.?

You helped me to eliminate the only thing standing in my way.

Foolish, hippie scum.

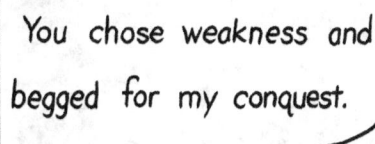

You chose weakness and begged for my conquest.

low no one can oppose
ie.

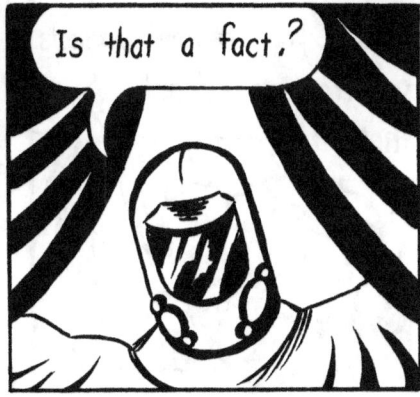

Is that a fact.?

Casey Bohn

PRESIDENT X

PRESIDENT X

25

Casey Bohn

nd I would have taken im with me.

And his body would be intact.

PROOF!

PROOF that we are not alone.

Gone—thanks to you.

Nice shootin', Tex.

Casey Bohn

PERRY BLOOM: ANIMAL DEALER

Casey Bohn

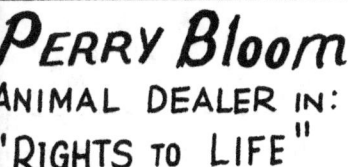

PERRY Bloom
ANIMAL DEALER IN:
"RIGHTS TO LIFE"

by Casey Bohn

Ugh... I **still** can't believe Disney owns likeness rights to polar bears.

Well, they **do** own every living polar bear.

And they've got to afford to keep their habitat at negative sixty some-how. Why not merchandising?

Still, like, don't you think it's kind of...not right?

Yeah, I guess...

Entitled little brat.

33

ADVERTISING

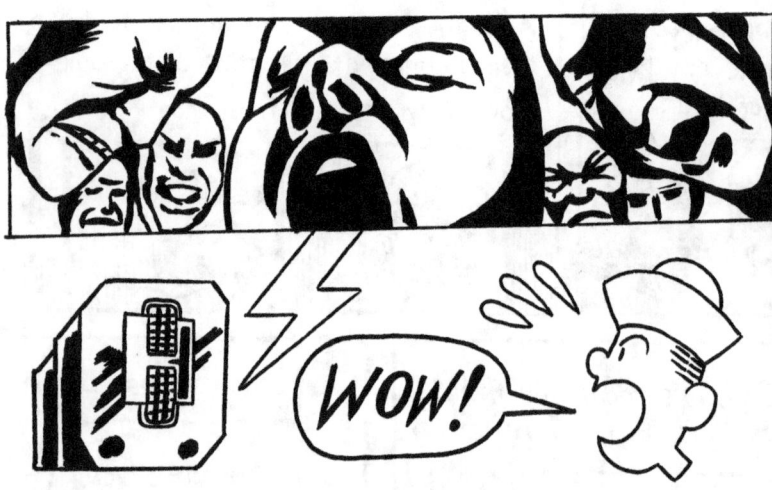

ADVERTISING

Casey Bohn

Casey Bohn

Great show today, Haroo!

Thanks, Mr. President.

THE SLEEP RACKET

Casey Bohn

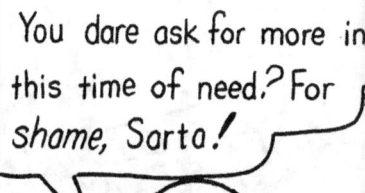

THE SLEEP RACKET

DEPARTMENT OF ARITHMETEK

There's an extra sleep ticket for you if you show me the camp payroll.

MYSQL...6
HANIT...4
BOYL...3

ME...12 NX...9
RD... MI...2
HP   .3
         9

I KNEW IT!

The President has been stealing sleep from everyone!

Print me a hard copy of this, willya?

Casey Bohn

ADVERTISING

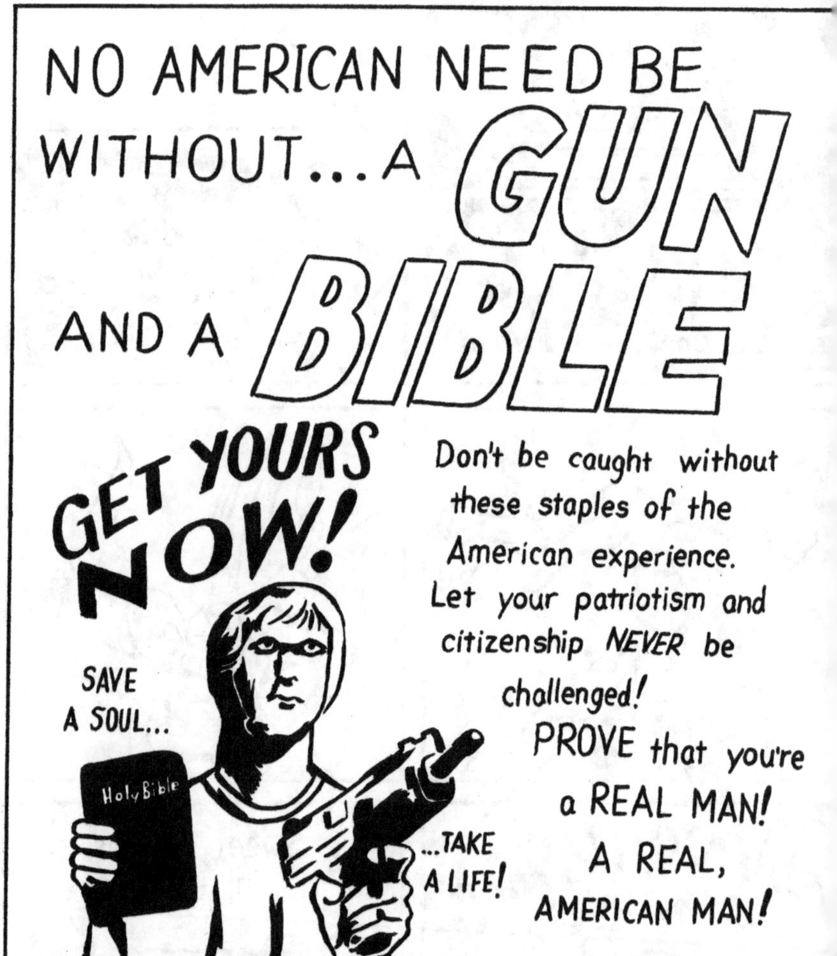